SOFIA MARTINEZ

My Vida LoCA

by Jacqueline Jules

illustrated by Kim Smith

PICTURE WINDOW BOOKS
a capstone imprint

Sofia Martinez is published by
Picture Window Books, a Capstone Imprint
1710 Roe Crest Drive
North Mankato, MN 56003
www.mycapstone.com

Library of Congress Cataloging-in
Publication Data
Jules, Jacqueline, 1956- author.
My vida loca / by Jacqueline Jules;
illustrated by Kim Smith.
pages cm. -- (Sofia Martinez)

Summary: Sofia's adventures and disasters
continue in this compilation of three
previously published books.

ISBN 978-1-4795-8720-9 (pbk.)
ISBN 978-1-4795-8721-6 (ebook pdf)

1. Hispanic American children--Juvenile
fiction. 2. Hispanic American families--
Juvenile fiction. 3. Humorous stories.
[1. Hispanic Americans--Fiction. 2. Family
life--Fiction. 3. Humorous stories.] I. Smith,
Kim, 1986- illustrator. II. Title. III. Series:
Jules, Jacqueline, 1956- Sofia Martinez.

PZ7.J92947Myk 2016
[E]--dc   232015025503

Designer: Kay Fraser

Printed in the United States of America in
North Mankato, Minnesota.
042016   009746R

TABLE OF CONTENTS

CHAPTER 1

The Best Gift

It was Christmas! Sofia and her family headed to her abuela's house to open gifts. Sofia's cousin Hector and his family came too.

Mamá and Papá gave Sofia a board game. It looked fun, but it was not what Sofia was hoping for.

Her sisters, Elena and Luisa,

gave Sofia a pink sweater.

"¡Bonito!" Sofia said. "¡Gracias!"

It still wasn't the present Sofia

was dreaming of.

Abuela handed a box to Sofia.

"Here you go, my sweet Sofia."

Sofia tore off the wrapping paper
and squealed with joy.

"A Superstar Sing Box!" she yelled.

Sofia picked up the microphone and sang while the rest of her family opened presents.

"¡Feliz Navidad! ¡Feliz Navidad!"

Sofia sang the song five times in a row.

She was ready to sing it again when Mamá interrupted.

"No más música, Sofia. Sit down for Christmas dinner," she said.

After dessert, Sofia picked up her microphone again.

Elena and Luisa groaned. Baby Mariela put her hands over her ears and cried.

Tía Carmen grabbed Mariela.

Tío Miguel rushed to get their

coats. Hector and his brothers were

leaving, too!

"Don't go!" Sofia cried. "I want to sing for you. You can even sing *with* me if you want."

"Maybe tomorrow," Hector said as he waved. "¡Hasta luego!"

CHAPTER 2

Nonstop Singing

Early the next morning, Sofia tiptoed downstairs with her singing machine.

She climbed onto the coffee table, using it as a stage. Sofia swayed and spun, pretending her nightgown was a fancy dress.

Sofia loved the sound of her voice through the microphone.

Mamá called down the stairs.

"¡No más música! The family is trying to sleep."

Sofia waited for Mamá and Papá to come down for breakfast. She had the microphone ready when they walked into the kitchen.

"¡Feliz Navidad! ¡Feliz Navidad!" Sofia sang loudly.

Papá rubbed his head. He didn't look excited. "That's the same song you sang last night."

"Yo sé," Sofia said. "It's my best one!"

"You know lots of songs," Mamá said. "What about "Los Pollitos" or "De Colores"?"

"Sometimes I forget the words," Sofia said.

"We can fix that," Mamá said. "Come with me to the piano."

Mamá and Sofia practiced until Sofia knew all the words.

"Gracias, Mamá. I'll go sing for Papá," Sofia said.

Papá was in the basement watching soccer. Sofia had to turn the volume up on her machine so Papá could hear her over the soccer match.

"Do you like my singing?" Sofia asked loudly.

"Sí," Papá said, his eyes on the screen. "The rest of the family should hear you, too. Go visit your cousin Hector."

"Good idea!" Sofia said.

She couldn't wait to sing all of her songs. She just needed an audience.

CHAPTER 3

A Place for a Star

Sofia carried her singing machine across the yard to her cousins' house. But as soon as she started singing, Tía Carmen stopped her.

"Ahora no, Sofia," she said. "Baby Mariela is taking her nap."

"You could sing outside," Hector said.

"Hace frío," Sofia said. "And I don't have my hat."

"It's not that cold out, and you can borrow one from Mamá."

Hector took a fluffy hat and leather gloves out of the closet.

"¡Elegante!" Sofia said. "With these on, I feel like a star."

"You look like one, too,"

Hector said.

Hector and Sofia went outside and stood on the corner with the Superstar Sing Box.

"I'll give a concert for the neighborhood," Sofia said.

One of the neighbors walked by with a dog. The dog sat down to sing with Sofia. "AROOO!"

Soon, another neighbor came by with a dog. "AROOO!"

"Sofia!" Hector shouted. "The dogs love you!"

Sofia had fun singing until a third dog came by. This one was bigger and had a very loud bark.

"ARF! ARF! ARF!"

Sofia couldn't hear her own voice anymore.

"¡Silencio!" she told the big dog.

But he was too excited to listen.

"ARF! ARF! ARF!"

Sofia frowned.

"I'm going inside!" she told Hector. "I'll sing for my sisters."

But Elena and Luisa were tired of listening to Sofia.

"Go see Abuela," Luisa said.

"She gave you the machine."

"¡Claro!" Sofia said.

A little while later, Sofia was at her abuela's house. She set up her machine.

Then she turned the volume up and sang loudly. Sofia smiled and swayed like she was on TV. She was a singing superstar!

Sofia sang and sang and sang.

She danced, too.

Abuela clapped and cheered.

"¡Maravilloso! Sing it again!"

Finally, Sofia had found the

perfect audience!

The
Secret
Recipe

CHAPTER 1

Cooking with Abuela

On Saturday afternoon, Sofia rushed over to Abuela's house.

Abuela was making arroz con leche for the church supper.

Sofia loved helping her abuela cook, and her abuela loved spending time with Sofia.

Abuela stirred the rice in a
giant pot. Sofia went to the pantry
to get the sugar.

"¡Cuidado!" Abuela called. "Be sure to get the container with the red lid, not the green one."

"I will," Sofia said.

Just then, the doorbell rang. It was the next door neighbor, Mrs. Flores.

"The special ingredient for your arroz con leche," Mrs. Flores said, handing over a small bag.

Sofia snuck around the corner

to listen. She was curious. What did

Abuela put in her rice pudding that

made it so special?

"Gracias," Abuela said. "I am glad you had some. I did not want to go shopping again."

Sofia quickly got bored and hurried back to the kitchen. She grabbed a container filled with white crystals.

She was not paying attention.

Her mind was still on that little

blue bag.

Sofia did not notice that she had taken the container with the green lid, not the red one.

"Add three cups of sugar to the pot!" Abuela called. She was still talking to Mrs. Flores.

Sofia was proud that Abuela trusted her to help.

"¡Muy bien!" she said when they were finished cooking.

"Would you like to take a little home for tomorrow's breakfast?" Abuela asked.

"Definitely!" Sofia said.

CHAPTER 2

The Mistake

The next morning, Sofia had breakfast with Mamá. They shared the arroz con leche.

"I can't wait to try it," Mamá said.

"Me, too," Sofia said. "I bet it's really good."

Sofia took a bite first. She made a face and spit it out.

"¿Qué pasa?" Mamá asked.

"Salty!" Sofia ran to the sink with a glass. "¡Agua!"

Sofia remembered going into the pantry the day before.

Abuela had warned her to get the jar with the red lid, not the green one. She had picked the wrong one!

"Oh, no! We need to make more pudding," Sofia said. "This time with sugar instead of salt."

"Sí," Mamá said. "I should have everything we need."

Mamá put rice, cinnamon sticks, milk, vanilla, and sugar on the kitchen counter. Sofia helped.

"Let's get cooking," Sofia said.

"It smells like you're making rice pudding," Papá said. He had just walked into the kitchen with Sofia's sisters.

"Only Abuela makes arroz con leche," Luisa said.

"Yo sé," Sofia explained. "This is an emergency."

Soon, the whole family was busy cooking.

Just as they were finishing, Sofia remembered something.

"We don't have the special ingredient!" she yelled.

Sofia told her family about the bag Mrs. Flores had brought over.

"Un misterio," Mamá said. "I'm not sure what it was."

"Will the arroz con leche still taste good?" Sofia asked.

"I hope so," Papá said.

"Me too," said Sofia quietly. "Me too."

CHAPTER 3

The Big Switch

Mamá put the arroz con leche into a serving pan to take to the church supper.

"We still have a problem," Luisa said. "Abuela will bring her pudding, too."

"That is a problem," Mamá said.

"We have to take her pan off

the table and put ours in its place,"

Elena said.

"No hay problema," Sofia said. "I'll keep her busy while Mamá makes the switch."

That night at the church, Sofia was nervous. As soon as she saw her abuela, Sofia ran toward her.

She pulled her grandmother's arm. "Will you come to the bathroom with me?" Sofia asked.

"¿Por qué?" Abuela asked.

"Por favor," Sofia pleaded.

Abuela was suspicious. "What's

going on?"

"Nada," Sofia said, trying to look innocent.

As Abuela turned around, she saw Mamá moving her arroz con leche off of the dessert table.

"Where are you going with my arroz con leche?" Abuela asked.

Sofia explained her mistake and how her family tried to help her fix it.

"I feel awful," Sofia said.

Abuela laughed. "You wanted to protect my feelings!"

"¡Claro!" Sofia said. "I love you!"

"Te amo mucho," Abuela said. "That's why I didn't say anything about your mistake. I didn't want to hurt your feelings."

"You knew?" Sofia asked.

"I had some for breakfast," Abuela said, smiling. "I made another pan after my first bite."

"I'm sorry I ruined our first pan," Sofia said. "I should have been more careful."

"It's okay, my dear," Abuela said. "It happens to every good cook."

"Even you?" Sofia asked.

"Even me," Abuela said, smiling. "I have messed up too many recipes to count!"

"And now we have two pans of pudding," Mamá said.

"But they are not the same," Sofia said. "Abuela has a secret ingredient in hers."

"What is this secret ingredient?" Mamá asked.

"Lemon peel," Abuela said.

"And love," Sofia said. "Lots and lots of love."

CHAPTER 1

A New Chore

Sofia dragged the feather duster over the coffee table. It was her job to dust. Elena swept the floors. Luisa emptied the trash.

"Every Saturday morning it's the same thing," Sofia moaned. "Chores are so boring."

"I'm tired of dusting," Sofia
told Papá. "Can I please have a
different job today?"

"Why don't you wash the car
instead? I'll dust," he said.

"¡Fantástico!" Sofia said.

Papá took Sofia outside and helped her fill a bucket with soap and water. He gave her a big yellow sponge.

"First scrub off the dirt. Then spray the car with the hose," he said.

"¡Perfecto!" Sofia said. "Spraying will be the best part!"

Papá pointed at the marigold garden next to the driveway.

"Be careful around the flowers," he said. "I planted those on Mother's Day for Mamá."

"¡Claro!" Sofia promised. "I will be extra careful."

Sofia got busy right away. She dunked the sponge and scrubbed. Dunk and scrub. Dunk and scrub.

Her cousin Hector ran over to help.

"Your car looks like it's covered in whipped cream," he said.

"Yo sé," Sofia said as she giggled. "Maybe it's time I sprayed."

She went to get the hose while Hector picked up the sponge.

When Sofia came back, Hector was leaning down, soaping the front wheel.

"¡Cuidado!" she grinned as she

started spraying the hose at him.

As Hector jumped to get out of the way, he bumped the side mirror. "Ouch!"

Sofia dropped the hose. "Are you okay?"

Hector rubbed his arm. "I am, but the mirror isn't."

"Oh, no! You broke it!" she shouted.

CHAPTER 2

Trouble

Sofia and Hector ran to the house. Luisa and Elena heard the noise and met them at the door.

"¡Ayúdanos!" Sofia cried.

"What did you do?" Elena asked.

"¡Rápido!" Sofia yelled.

When they got back to the car, there was even more trouble. A big stream of water was flowing across the driveway, right into Mamá's flower garden.

"Oh, no! I left the water running!" Sofia screamed.

"Mamá's marigolds!" Luisa said.

Sofia hurried to shut the water off. The yellow flowers looked like they were swimming.

Using her hands, Sofia pushed water out of the garden. Luisa, Elena, and Hector tried to help.

After a while, the garden wasn't flooded. But the flowers were still really droopy.

"We need more dirt," Luisa said.

"Mamá keeps big bags for planting by the side of the house," Sofia said.

"¡Vámonos!" Elena said.

Together, they dragged the heavy bags back to the flower garden and ripped them open.

They spread dirt until every
marigold stood up straight again.

"That looks a lot better," Sofia
said.

"But we don't!" Hector said.

They stared at each other. Their faces, hands, and clothes were all covered in mud.

"Now we have another mess to clean up," Sofia said.

CHAPTER 3

A Muddy Mess

Just then, Papá came outside.

"¿Qué pasa?" he asked.

"I dropped the hose and flooded the flowers," Sofia said.

"Oh, Sofia," he said.

"We also broke the mirror on the car," Sofia said, near tears.

Her heart thumped as Papá looked at the mirror.

"Lo siento," Sofia said quietly.

Papá simply pushed the folded mirror back into place and smiled.

"You fixed it!" Hector clapped.

Papá laughed. "The mirror was never broken. It was made to swing in and out."

"Thank goodness," Sofia said.

"Will the flowers be okay?'
Luisa asked.

Papá checked. "Sí. You did a
good job saving them."

"Gracias," Sofia held out her
arms to hug Papá. He stepped back
and grinned.

"I don't need to get dirty, too,"
he said.

Sofia looked at her muddy

clothes, then over at Hector, Elena,

and Luisa.

"We definitely need a bath!"

Luisa said.

"Or a shower," Sofia said as she

turned on the faucet.

Elena and Luisa squealed as
Sofia pointed the sprayer at them.

"Move away from the garden,"
she warned, smiling.

"Don't forget that the car needs a shower, too," Papá said.

"Sí, Papá," laughed Sofia. "And don't forget to dust!"

Spanish Glossary

abuela — grandma

agua — water

ahora no — not now

arroz con leche — rice pudding

ayúdanos — help us

bonito — pretty

claro — of course

cuidado — careful

elegante — elegant

fantástico — fantastic

Feliz Navidad — Merry Christmas

gracias — thank you

hace frío — it's cold

hasta luego — see you later

lo siento — I'm sorry

mamá — mom

maravilloso — marvelous

muy bien — very good

nada — nothing

no hay problema — no problem

no más música — no more music

papá — dad

perfecto — perfect

por favor — please

por qué — why

qué pasa — what's wrong

rápido — quick

sí — yes

silencio — silence

te amo mucho — I love you so much

tía — aunt

tío — uncle

un misterio — a mystery

vámonos — let's go

yo sé — I know

About the Author

Jacqueline Jules is the award-winning author of twenty-five children's books, including *No English* (2012 Forward National Literature Award), *Zapato Power: Freddie Ramos Takes Off* (2010 CYBILS Literary Award, Maryland Blue Crab Young Reader Honor Award, and ALSC Great Early Elementary Reads), and *Freddie Ramos Makes a Splash* (named on 2013 List of Best Children's Books of the Year by Bank Street College Committee).

When not reading, writing, or teaching, Jacqueline enjoys time with her family in Northern Virginia.

About the Illustrator

Kim Smith has worked in magazines, advertising, animation, and children's gaming. She studied illustration at the Alberta College of Art and Design in Calgary, Alberta.

Kim is the illustrator of the middle-grade mystery series The Ghost and Max Monroe, the picture book *Over the River and Through the Woods*, and the cover of the middle-grade novel *How to Make a Million*. She resides in Calgary, Alberta.

See you soon!

¡Nos vemos pronto!